MILLIE MORGAN, PIRATE

Landlubbers beware! Millie Morgan, pirate, has hung up her sea boots and is coming ashore!

Margaret Ryan has written many popular books for young readers. These include The *Fat Witch Rides Again* and the King Tubbitum stories, a number of which have been broadcast on the children's television programme, *Playdays*. She has a large Airedale dog and lives in Scotland.

Caroline Church also has a dog, whose name is Sally Two Shoes. While Caroline works in her studio in an old Oxfordshire mill, producing illustrations for children's books and for advertising, Sally sits on the windowsill watching a pig called Betty!

Some other titles

Art, You're Magic!
by Sam McBratney

Beware Olga!
by Gillian Cross

Holly and the Skyboard
by Ian Whybrow

Jolly Roger
by Colin McNaughton

Little Luis and the Bad Bandit
by Ann Jungman

Pappy Mashy
by Kathy Henderson

The Snow Maze
by Jan Mark

Tillie McGillie's Fantastical Chair
by Vivian French

The Unknown Planet
by Jean Ure

MARGARET RYAN

MILLIE MORGAN PIRATE

Illustrations by
Caroline Church

WALKER BOOKS
AND SUBSIDIARIES
LONDON • BOSTON • SYDNEY

For Johnnie with love

First published 1992 by
Walker Books Ltd, 87 Vauxhall Walk
London SE11 5HJ

This edition published 1994

6 8 10 9 7 5

Printed in England

British Library Cataloguing in Publication Data
A catalogue record for this book
is available from the British Library.

ISBN 0-7445-3095-4

Contents

JUST DROPPING IN

"Heave to. Heave three. Drop the anchor. Drop everything!" yelled Millie Morgan, pirate captain (retired).

"Pardon?" said Griffon, her vulture and first mate. "If you want me to bring the *Seabird* to a standstill, why can't you just say STOP, Millie?"

But Millie Morgan, pirate captain (retired), wasn't listening. She was peering through her telescope at the nearest bit of dry land.

"Well, stab me vitals and loosen me corset," she said. "This telescope isn't working. I can hardly see a thing."

"That's because you've parked your bubble gum on the fat end again," said Griffon.

He peeled it off, and Millie said, "AAR. AAR AAR.

AAR AAR AAR,"

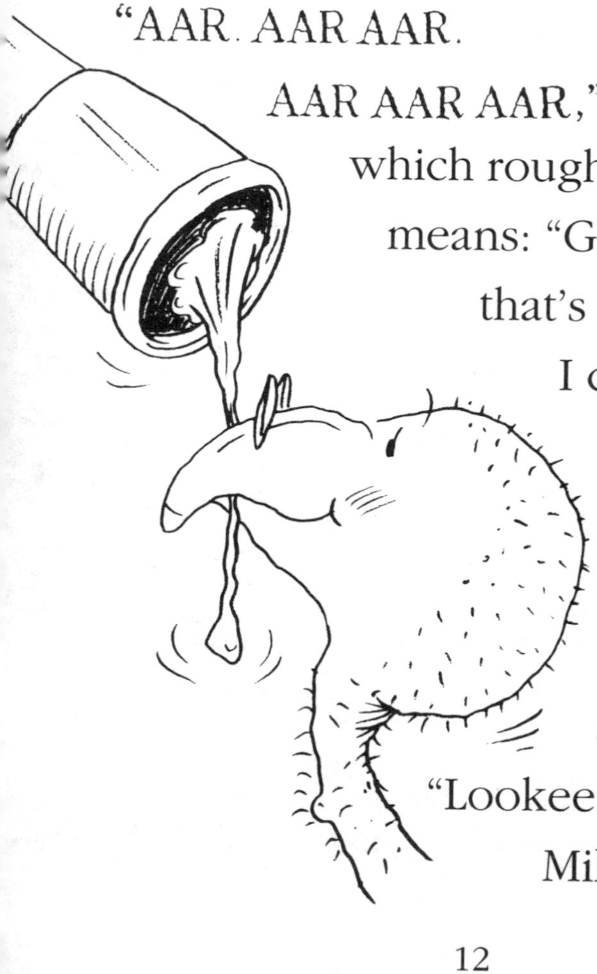

which roughly translated means: "Gosh, Griffon, that's much better. I can see now. Thanks very much."

"You're welcome," said Griffon.

"Lookee here, Griff," Millie went on.

"Now that the rest of the crew have retired ashore, I think it's time we settled down too. Take a look at Little Drowsing by the Sea.

Isn't it peaceful? My old bones tell me it's the perfect place for us."

Griffon looked.

"Perfect? It's perfectly awful. There are no cool cafés, no all-night chip shops, not even a take-away.

And with Cookie gone ashore now too, I don't know if my stomach can stand any more of your cooking."

"Now don't get in a miff, Griff. Cast your eye over yonder to the harbour wall. What do you see there?"

Griffon cast his eye. "I see an old inn with very few walls and even less roof. I see a ruin."

"Isn't it wonderful?" said Millie. "Once we've fixed it up, it'll be just right for us to retire to."

"But Little Drowsing doesn't even have a hot dog stand," said Griffon. "Without Cookie I'll starve."

"I'll still cook for you," said Millie.

"I think I'd rather starve," said Griffon.

IN A MESS

Millie bought the old inn from Mr Rookem, the estate agent in the high street. Griffon sighed as Millie handed over three large bags of gold doubloons in exchange for the keys. Not that they needed keys.

They could walk in through
the holes in the walls

or fly in through the holes
in the roof.

But Millie was happy. She skipped about when she saw the inside of the inn.

"This be grand, Griffy," she said.

Griffon shook his bald head. "This be very far from grand, Millie. This be a right old mess."

"Keep your wig on, Griffy old mate. We'll soon have it all shipshape. Everything we need to fix the inn is on board the *Seabird.* Fly me over there and we'll start work right away."

They began by flying planks of wood and buckets of nails over from the ship, and before long the D.I.Y. pirate was noticed in Little Drowsing.

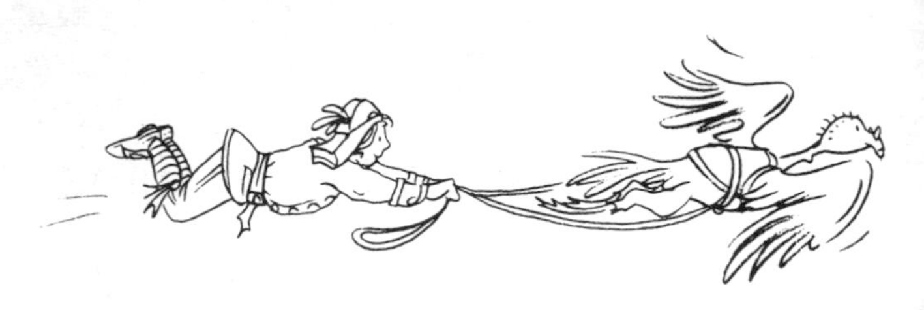

"That's her. That's Millie Morgan, the fierce pirate," spluttered nosy Mrs Whinge, the postmistress, to nosy Mr Carp, the bank manager.

"I've just found out from Mr Rookem that she's bought The Old Inn. She's going to retire there. We must put a stop to that right away. We don't want *her* sort living in Little Drowsing."

"Quite right," said Mr Carp. "But let's move her on *after* she's rebuilt The Old Inn. She and that big bird are doing a good job. The old place looks better already."

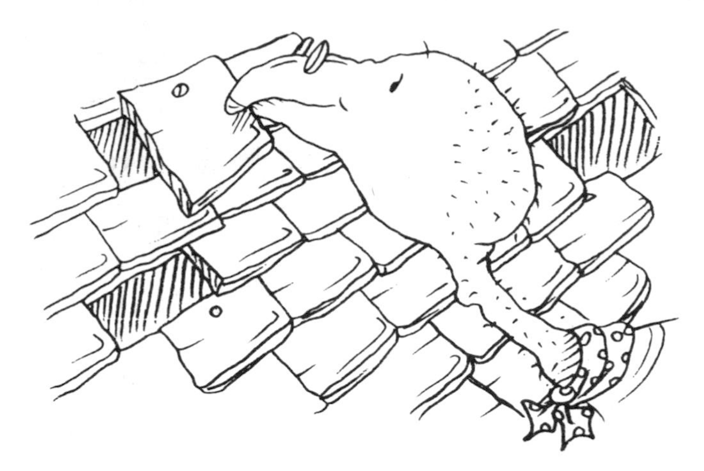

And it did. Millie built up the walls while Griffon patched up the roof, and soon the inn was wind and watertight. Then Millie put up a fence and a little white gate.

"It's looking good, Griffy old mate. Just the skull and crossbone curtains to hang up now. I'll do that while you fly over to the *Seabird* and bring back the brass cannon and the special ammunition."

"Expecting trouble, Millie?" asked Griffon.

"Well," said Millie. "I've noticed some lace curtains a-twitching and some beady eyes a-peering, and my old pirate bones tell me there's something afoot."

"You and your bones," muttered Griffon, but he went to collect the cannon and the special ammunition. Millie's bones were seldom wrong.

THE PIRATES
MOVE IN

Millie and Griffon were sitting by a roaring fire toasting their toes and cracking their jaws on the disgusting beef stew Millie had made. She really was the worst cook in the world. Who else would make fish finger and treacle sandwiches

or bake spaghetti and spinach cakes?

Griffon bravely swallowed a beakful of stew and felt it thud into his stomach.

"Where have your spare seaboots gone, Millie?" he asked. "Are they in this stew?"

"Don't be daft, Griffy," said Millie. But she did wonder. She'd had to take the ship's axe to the meat to cut it up.

"If only Cookie were here," she sighed. "If only he hadn't retired to cook in that fancy restaurant. If only he were here to make us his steaming beef hotpot with fluffy, floury dumplings."

"And crunchy roast potatoes," said Griffon.

"And ice-cream gateau," said Millie.

"On a separate plate," said Griffon.

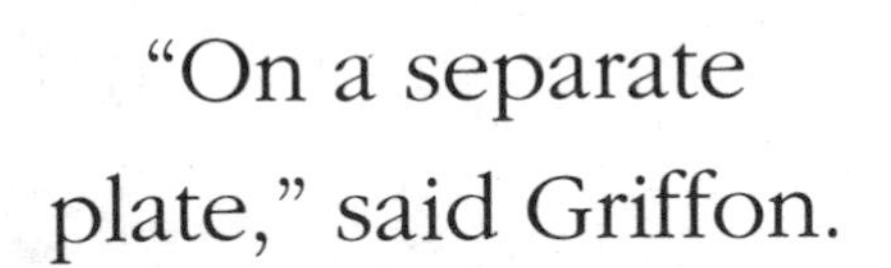

"Mmmmmmmm," they both said. "Delicious."

Suddenly there was a sharp rap on the front door.

"Who can that be?" wondered Griffon.

Millie stood up and her bones creaked. "My old bones tell me that be trouble."

"Stop listening to your old bones and open the door."

Millie did. Mrs Whinge and Mr Carp stood on the doorstep.

"We've brought a petition signed by a great many people in Little Drowsing," said Mrs Whinge. "They don't want the likes of you living here. They want you to leave."

"Leave?" Millie cried. "But I've only just got here. I've retired here. Scraped all the barnacles off me bottom and hung up me seaboots."

Mr Carp looked at Millie's bare toes.

"So I see," he said. "But you're not welcome. We don't want your sort here. So pack up your belongings and we'll be here first thing in the morning to see that you leave."

And Mrs Whinge and Mr Carp smiled nastily and left.

Millie showed the petition to Griffon. "Shivering shellfish," she said. "What a lot of people want us to go."

Griffon read the petition carefully all the way through, and he gave a hearty laugh. “Don’t be a silly, Millie. That horrible pair have made this up between them. Just read the names.”

Millie read the names.

Mrs Whinge
Mr Carp
Mr Whinge
Mrs Carp
Miss Whinge
Etta Carp
Master Whinge
Netta Carp
Rover Whinge
Tweetie Pie Carp
Tiddles Whinge
Goldie Carp

"Right, Griffy," said Millie. "Look out the special ammunition for the cannon. When that pair come round in the morning we'll be ready for them. Nobody messes with Millie Morgan and gets away with it."

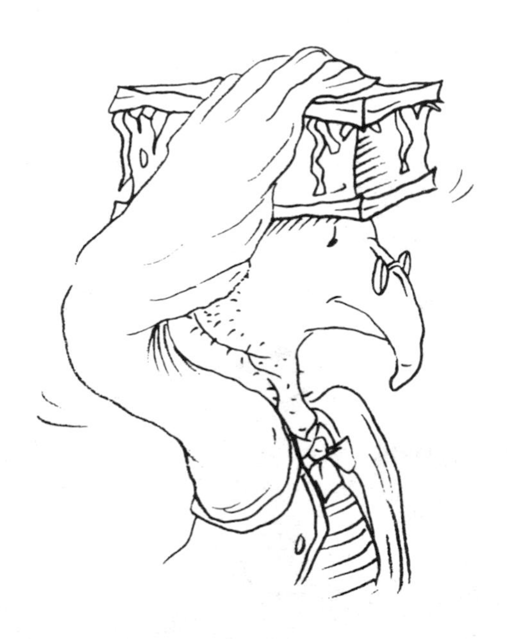

IN THE MORNING
Ammunition

Morning came early as usual, but Millie was up waiting for it, and Mrs Whinge and Mr Carp.

"Well," they said, marching up the path, "are you ready to leave?"

"Certainly not," said Millie. "But I think you might be. You can't fool Millie Morgan with your dirty tricks.

Load the cannon, Griffy and shiver their timbers! Wizzard their gizzards! Avast with the blast!"

Griffon sighed. "How about FIRE, Millie," he said.

"FIRE, MILLIE!" yelled Millie.

Griffon fired and millions of mouldy fish finger and treacle sandwiches, and stringy spaghetti and spinach cakes rained down on Mrs Whinge and Mr Carp.

"Wowwwwwwl!" yelled Mr Carp.

"Owwwww!" yelled Mrs Whinge.

"And there's plenty more where those came from if you two ever come visiting again!" yelled Millie, as they ran off down the path.

COOK IN

They were just going back indoors when a face peered over the fence. It had treacle and fish fingers stuck to its nose, and bits of spaghetti and spinach hanging from its pirate's hat.

"Cookie," yelled Millie. "You're back." And she ran and kissed him. *SSSSSSSSSSSLLLLLLLLLLOOO*
OOOOOOOOOOOOOOOOOOO
RRRRRRRRRRRRRRRRPPPPPP.

"Didn't like that fancy restaurant," said Cookie when he'd recovered. "Do you know, they wouldn't let me wear my pirate's hat in the kitchen? So I left and set off to find you.

Luckily I knew which way you were headed. I came round the corner just as the cannon fired the special ammunition. Then I knew I was home. Can I come and cook for you?"

"Of course," said Millie. "We could set up a fancy restaurant here, and call it The Jolly Lodger. That way you could wear your pirate's hat wherever you liked."

THE
JOLLY LODGER
INN

So that's what they did, and soon the restaurant became famous for miles around. To get in you had to come dressed as a pirate. The people of Little Drowsing thought this was great fun.

But one night two really fierce-looking pirates turned up. They wore black eye patches and big black beards.

They thought nobody would recognize them under all that, but Millie would have known Mrs Whinge and Mr Carp anywhere.

"Ah, here be two really fierce pirates. We don't usually let your sort in, but if you promise to behave..."

Mrs Whinge and Mr Carp coughed and shuffled and they promised they would.

Millie held in a giggle as she served them large pirate-sized helpings of steaming beef hotpot.

After that, Mrs Whinge and Mr Carp came to the restaurant every Friday night. No one could resist Cookie's wonderful food.

Millie was delighted at how well things had turned out. "I knew this was the perfect place for us, Griffy," she said. "My old bones told me so."

But Griffon didn't reply. It's rude to speak with your mouth full.